# Rh Negative...What are we?

## True Accounts of UFO's, Astral Projection, Murder & Supernatural Phenomenon

By Stephanie Wolfe

# Contents

Night of Creatures

Disturbance

Haunted

Triangle

Blackout

Total Darkness

The Devil's Number

Fukushima: Daiichi Nuclear Catastrophe Update

The Historical Use of Fluoride and The Current Controversies Behind It

The Doorways of the Mind

*Dedicated to*

*P. Wolfe, K. Jimenez &*

*Joshua Jimenez*

*my three-favorite people in this whole world. You inspire me to be my best every day.*

# Preface

This book is going to reveal truths to you, truths you may not be ready for. It is the red pill that Neo takes in the Matrix. I plan to write a sequel to cover and connect the dots that I have laid out in this first book. I have discovered so much more since writing this and have so much more to share with my readers. These stories are all true. They are original because they are true. This book is to give comfort to those who have had similar experiences. They have either happened to me or my family, in some cases I even held back. My parents noted this and reminded me of many details I missed. I plan on covering these in the upcoming sequel. This book is not just for Rh Negative people, I wrote it to be entertaining for anyone, so please do not feel like you are excluded if you are not Rh negative. There are two more blood types that are even more rare than Rh negatives, such as "golden blood", now if you have that then you are officially special, at least medically. But you do not have to have special blood to be amazing, as most amazing people are probably not Rh negative. This book simply points out very strange experiences that have happened to Rh negative people and makes the claim that Rh negative people are prone to supernatural experiences.

It is thought that Rh Negative people are only about 15% of the entire population. O negatives are universal donors and AB negatives the rarest of Rh negatives, are the universal receivers.

I have had a remarkably strange life; I suspect it is because I am Rh negative; my blood type is AB negative. My great grandparents were first cousins and I am royal blooded on both sides of my family. My parents are distant cousins as well. My mother and my father originate from the Iberian regions of northern Spain. My siblings and mother are Rh negative too, but they are O negative.

I once had a crazy religious woman tell me someone who was related to me offered me up to Satan while I was in the womb. I sometimes wonder about that because I am a Capricorn (sign of the devil) born on January 17, (a day that is the birthday of many historically intense people: Benjamin Franklin, Mohammed Ali, Jim Carrey to name a few) it is also a triple birthday in my immediate family. The odds of that happening are astronomical, it cannot be meaningless. My name Stephanie is Greek for crowned and illuminated one. It gets weirder…follow me down the rabbit hole.

It is said that royals were cannibals. Many historians and paintings testify to this. Cannibalism leads to blood disorders. Royals once worshipped the lion, because it used to be at the top of the food chain. That is why we so often see the lion in royal art. It is also the reason the royals became human blood drinking vampiric cannibals. Even today the elite that run our media are constantly inundating us with cannibalism. In the form of TV shows, movies, zombie walks and in the media we see videos and reports of 'spirit cooking' in which humans are laid out nude on dinner tables. Pop stars makes music videos toying with the idea of eating people. Like attracts like. Blood attracts similar blood. There is power in it, and the royals knew it. The Aztecs and so many other cultures knew it too, which it why human blood has been used as spiritual and now more recently biological currency. There is data now that claims transfusions to the old with young blood has rejuvenating effects on older bodies. The royals ate human flesh to become like the lion, to properly and to officially show their superiority by positioning themselves officially at the top of the food chain. That is why the Egyptian sphinx has the body of the lion and head of a human.

It is speculated by many that the lost tribes of Israel went to Europe and are the origins of many royal families. That would also explain the excessive use of the lion as their symbol. According to research into my family tree my own family comes from the tribe of Simeon.

There are many medical rarities in my family. I have anemia and am extraordinarily deathly allergic to many things including birth control pills, latex, spermicide, and "lifesaving" Benadryl which nearly killed me. I am also highly allergic to gold. My mother who is O negative, is allergic to Aloe vera and penicillin she was also born with a caul, a type of uterine veil or lining which is said to be extremely rare and comes with it many international superstitions. Though it is rare, many prominent historical figures were born with a caul. Most lore sees it as a sign of power, sometimes sailors would buy them and keep them for good luck and protection while at sea.

In my family we are mostly Rh negative and red hair is dominant. My own hair is reddish dark brown. My eyes are very dark with a slight grey tinged ring and change to black when I am angry. I was born peculiarly strong. The day I was born I rolled over twice, back to back, shocking the medical staff (most babies roll over at between 4-6 months.) but now I consider myself fragile. Now as an adult my mind is still strong, but my body is weaker. I have always been pulled to dark and mysterious conversations. Curious about religion and the occult by the age of 8 years old (though I am not a practitioner). I have always been nocturnal, and always have more energy at night. This is common for Rh negative people; I believe it is because we are more sensitive to the sun effects on our melatonin/serotonin levels. I am powerfully creative. I write, sing, act and my siblings and I have won numerous awards for our artistic contributions in writing, painting, and music. We also have alarmingly accurate highly psychic dreams and are very intuitive. Even children in our family have prophetic dreams.

I have so many odd stories to tell and I firmly believe it is because Rh negative people are unique not superior, just different. There was a study about how radiosensitivity is different in Rh negative people versus Rh positive people. Radiation is much more destructive to mammals versus reptiles, and amphibians. Could it be the lack of this protein in our bloods might be a good thing when it comes to radiation?

Here is a quote from the study findings (Electron Physician. 2016 Aug; 8(8): 828–832. Published online 2016 Aug 25. doi: 10.19082/2828 PMCID: PMC5053467 PMID: 27757196 'Rh factor is associated with individual radiosensitivity: A cytogenetic study' Meysam Khosravifarsani,1 Ali Shabestani Monfared,2 and Sajad Borzoueisileh3, Fair Use) conclusion #5:

"The present study suggested that chromosomal radiosensitivity of lymphocytes in normal individuals with Rh+ factor is higher than their Rh− counterparts. However, this difference is not generalized to other types of cells. This finding revealed that the Rh factor can be considered one of the hereditary traits affecting individuals' radiosensitivity and can be a valuable item in radiation protection regulations. However, further in-vivo and in-vitro studies are needed for validation."

Protein is sensitive to radiation, it's not formal but we all notice this when we attempt to cook meat in our microwaves. In the study they used two different types of radiation and studied the before and after of many different types of cells and cell reproduction. There was a slight difference to how sensitive the two blood groups recovered from it. More research should be done on this for us to truly see more clear differences, but it is fascinating that there is a difference. Here is a link address to the study: https://www.ncbi.nlm.nih.gov/pmc/articles/PMC3920532/

All of these stories are absolutely true. The frightful situations these people are in have happened either around me or to someone in my immediate family. I have changed the names in them, including my own but know they are all very personal to me, and very distressing. It is difficult to think about some of what is in this book. To speak of them in person makes me nervous, but it does feel like I am surrendering them. Giving up the burden that some of them have left, by sharing them in this way. In my everyday life I would say I am quite the coward. I don't play with Ouija boards, nor can I handle scary movies other than PG13 rated films. I imagine you will be wondering if I exaggerated or embellished these in any way, please know that I did not. The experiences are not just based on true stories. They are true stories. The scary details are accurate in their descriptions. I could leave you with something like, "I hope you enjoy this book." before you begin to read it but that's not true. The truth is I hope this book scares you. I hope it makes you realize life is not as simple as we want it to be. I hope it makes you safer and more cautious at night. I hope it makes you double check your locks before you go to bed. Know that life is full of mystery and is so much eerier than we generally think it is. At the very least, let it be a reminder that anything is possible.

If you are Rh negative you might be destined for an extraordinary life filled with exceptional experiences but remember you are not alone. After the stories are additional reports I included that tie into conspiracy, what we've learned from history on the radiosensitivity of animals especially on mammals, and an exploration of hypnosis. I truly hope you enjoy them. If you wish to contact me and share a personal experience with me, I would very much welcome that.

# The Night of Creatures

It was a cooler than usual night in southern California. The evening had started out pretty fun. I, Lisa along with my college friends Scott and Natalie had just gotten some fast food. After wasting time, walking around the mall buying random stupid stuff. We were laughing and listening to pop music in the car as I pulled into the apartment complex.

Now, when I happen to see something truly scary…I don't scream. I get tongue-tied, I lose my voice. I wish I had been able to stop the goofiness in the car for a second but when I saw it, my heart stopped, and I couldn't speak. There at night, in my parking spot, I saw the lower half of a pale almost white creature with a long-curled tail, crawl into the small bush next to my parking space. It was similar to a hairless cat except the hind legs and feet were huge. The skin looked very thick and a bit shiny but so pale like an albino elephant. I only saw the lower half which was about one and half foot across. The hind feet were the size of a large dog, like a German shepherd. The tail was thick and had to be long because it was curved into a perfect large spiral like a snail shell, the diameter was about ten inches across. It looked like a powerful strong tail, one that could cause pain if used as a weapon.

It seemed startled by my head lights and stood half hidden by the bush for a full two seconds, before it crawled fully into the bush. The spine was odd too, it didn't go across like a dog it was at an angle rising higher towards the head, more like a kangaroo vertebra.

I had stopped singing and laughing and talking. My friends Scott and Natalie hadn't seen it. I kept my eyes on the bush waiting to see it come out. I have a fear of wild animals attacking me in the night. I mean, doesn't everybody? I can't be the only one.

Anyway, they gathered their bags and as they were about to get out of the car my voice came back, "Don't go out there!" I blurted. "Why? What is it?", they asked me confused. "I don't know…I saw something…it was crazy looking. It's hiding in the bush. Did you guys see it, when I pulled in to park my car?"

"Is it still in the bush?" Scott sounded intrigued. "Yes, I haven't taken my eyes off it this whole time. I am waiting for it to leave. I don't know how it's hiding in that small bush. It's too big to fit in there! It's like the size of a goat!" The bush was one square foot and sixteen inches high. The creature I saw should have needed three bushes in a row to hide completely. Scott got out of my car unafraid, "Let's check it out! I wanna see it!"

"Oh, my God! Scott don't!" Natalie begged. Out of all of us she was the youngest and most sensitive. "I'm not going out there. Lisa, what did it look like?" I tried to think of what I could compare it to, "It was kinda like a giant hairless cat, but scarier. It had a long tail and he curled it in and hid in the bush, it stopped for a second then, walked in the bush. I've never seen anything like it. It's hind feet and legs were really big, like a dog's."

When Scott got out of the car for some reason I felt braver, so I got out too. We stood in front of the small bush. "I don't understand. It can't be in there." I whined; the situation made me feel about five years old. Scott suggested mischievously, "What if it made itself invisible?" he smiled dramatically holding back his laughter, but I knew he actually meant it. Scott believed in any and every conspiracy theory and had no lack of imagination. I rolled my eyes, "It's not there…it just disappeared." Scott looked skeptical, "It didn't just disappear. I'm telling you it's still there." He seemed confident, like some kind of veteran vampire slayer or something. He pulled out his tactical knife. Without hesitation he stabbed it into the bush. I had stepped away from it, feeling skittish. "Did you hear that?" he bent down towards it.

"No. What?" I listened. He stabbed at the bush again, at what seemed like bare air in the bush. Then I heard it. I walked closer. It was a deep, powerful guttural growl coming straight from the bush. It was a growl I have never heard before. It sounded like a human voice expertly combined with a wild beast. It was coming from deep inside; it had an almost reverb to it. It was so edgy sounding; the pitch was so low. It, this thing was angry at us. We should have left, I should have gone upstairs then, with Natalie and our knick knacks we bought from the mall, but the sound was so incredible. The growls were louder than a dog's and there was an intelligence to them. This was like no thing I had ever heard or seen before. The large creature really was still in the bush, and Scott was right, incredibly, it had made itself invisible.

"Scott, I feel like this thing…it understands us. Everything we say. It doesn't feel like it's just an animal." "Let's trap it and sell it." He suggested. I shook my head, "No. let's just go inside now. We are pissing it off." Scott was still not worried. "Let's at least pepper spray it. Let's just see what it does." He looked over at Natalie who was clutching her shopping bags as if they were protecting her. "You okay?" he asked, she nodded yes.

I kept my eyes on the bush determined to see it again. Little lizards kept coming around us and around the bush. This surprised me as usually these lizards hide but that night they were all around us and the shrub, it was as if they knew the creature. I told Scott to get my pepper spray out of the car, and we made a deal to go inside after one more experiment.

Scott grabbed the pepper spray out of my purse and when he lifted his head out of the car he suddenly looked frozen. He saw something. "Look over there…do you see that?" I backed away from the plant, so I could see what he was looking at. About fifteen feet away behind a dumpster that was close by, stood something tall with huge hands. It's head was too big and shaped liked a stereotypical alien head, it's body was so thin, reminiscent of a flimsy stick figure. We stared at the distinct shadow. I thought maybe it was an illusion, but then the shadow's right hand opened and closed dramatically. Then it held its hand perfectly still, five fingers stretched out wide, in a frozen wave stance. It was showing off for us and wanted to make sure we saw it and knew it was real. I looked away. I told myself and Scott, "Not now Scott. Let's deal with one creepy thing at a time. Let's focus on the thing in the bush." Scott was not okay, he was disturbed and found it hard to look away from the menacing alien-like silhouette.

"They are connected Scott. Whatever this thing is and that thing standing over there is…they are together somehow. It's not a coincidence that both of these things are out tonight." Scott nodded in agreement, "Maybe this thing in the bushes is that thing's pet?" he suggested, "Maybe…" I agreed. We got in positions surrounding the hiding little monster and I sprayed it with pepper spray. The growls came again louder and louder. We could taste the pepper spray in the air and feel how it began to irritate our breathing and eyes. The wind had blown it back at our faces. I felt really stupid as I coughed and gagged on it. "That's it Scott. I'm done. I've had enough. It's not coming out." A part of me did want to see the creature again, this time in its entirety but I couldn't handle the tiny bits of pepper spray going into my throat.

Scott agreed it was time to give up, he too was coughing. He had seen the alien-shadow walk around and disappear as well across the parking lot. Natalie covered her nose and mouth and we grabbed our stuff running upstairs towards my apartment.

I researched other stories online, looking for similar descriptions of what I saw, and found one from Africa. It seemed to describe the same being and was given the label of 'hobgoblin'. In the story I found the African man had watched it go through his belongings and steal his pocket knife. Once it noticed he was watching it, it ran out of the open window giving him one final glance and snarl before jumping out of sight. It's face was demonic, not that of an animal's.

I noticed for a few days afterwards how many little lizards seemed to be attracted to that one spot, the area around the bush but within a week their behavior returned to normal.

*A photo from a conspiracy social media group very similar to 'hobgoblin'.*

# Disturbance

Marianne was an exuberant teenager, she loved fashion magazines, everyone else's hair except her own and cute nice boys. She, as well as most of her friends liked to babysit.

It was November that year in Duluth, Georgia. A lively city twenty minutes away from downtown Atlanta. There she was babysitting two small children for the Colburns, in their oversized townhouse style apartment. The Colburns were a pleasant family she knew from her church. They were going to a concert and would be staying in a luxury hotel, meaning that Marianne would be staying the night with the children and would be making tons of money. At least in her young eyes it seemed like a ton of money. She was excited to be away from her own annoying family and siblings. Babysitting felt like a paid vacation to her.

The children, Emma and Wes were six and four years old and were super cute and affectionate. They thought of Marianne as an older sister. Marianne texted her friends and made snacks until it was 8:00PM, bedtime. She changed the children into their footsy pajamas, brushed their teeth, read them a bedtime story, and tucked them in sweetly with a kiss on the cheek and warm smile, "Goodnight...sweet dreams. I'll see you in the morning, okay?" The sleepy children waved and yawned, closed their eyes peacefully drifting off to sleep in their cozy plush beds.

Marianne looked around at the Colburns movie collection and found a stack of blank DVD cases, with blank DVDs inside. Out of curiosity she popped one in, she quickly realized it was porn and popped it back out. The Colburns having sex or being sexual in anyway shocked her. She felt really bad, she had not meant to be nosy.

Eventually she found a cheesy romantic comedy and fell asleep texting her BFF, Kim Sullivan.

At 3:00AM something woke her up. The TV had turned itself off, some of the lights were still on but dimmed. Something disturbed her sleep, but what?

Then she heard it, a scream. A bloodcurdling scream. "AHHH! NO... STOP PLEASE!" It sounded like a young man. It was extremely loud. She heard footsteps outside. She was still groggy, but she stood up and looked out the window, not seeing anything. The screaming continued. "AHHHH!!!!NO!!!!!AHHHHH!!!!!" She had never ever heard a man scream out in pain like that before. She heard another voice, but it was harder to hear and understand. It sounded more like grunting versus talking.

The screams got closer. Outside the hallway was the apartment front door, it was a ground level, two-story unit. She heard footsteps running past the front door, there was panting. "AHHH!!! SOMEBODY PLEASE HELP ME!!!! PLEASE!" She grabbed her phone and dialed 911. "Hello 911 what is your emergency?" "Um…Yes, please send someone over right away there is a man screaming outside, he's being attacked." "Can you see him?" "No. I can only hear him. There is something else that is hurting him. I can hear it hurting him. Please hurry! I can't go help him I'm just a teenager and I am babysitting."

"Yes, do not go outside. You are the third person to call with the same complaint. Stay where you are. Do not go outside. I am sending someone over to you right now. Give me your address." Marianne was shaking, she gave her the address then hung up. The screams were getting louder and louder.

Closer and closer. "Somebody…please help me!" The voice was outside the Colburns door. "He's going to kill me." She wished she had a gun.

Maybe if she had a gun she could help him. She felt so helpless. She slowly stepped closer to the door. She looked out the peephole. There was a young black man without a shirt on, he had blood everywhere dripping. He was knocking on the doors in the hallway frantically trying to open them, knocking on them, then turning to try another door. Her view was blurry. He came to the Colburn's door, shook the doorknob, and knocked. "Is somebody in there? Please open up. I'm going to die if you don't let me in. Please! Please help me!"

She called out through the door. "Yes, I'm here. I called 911. They are sending the police now. They'll be here soon! You are gonna be safe!"

Just then, little Wes came downstairs. "Marianne, I'm thirsty. Can I have some milk?" Marianne jumped out of her skin, startled! "Oh, sure sweetie. Go back to bed and I will bring up a glass okay?" "Okay…" he yawned, and pitter patted his way back up the stairs. She ran to the kitchen and grabbed a glass, poured some milk in it, and ran upstairs. Calmly, she gave Wes his glass of milk and left the hall light on for him. "Wes, just put it on the night table when you're done okay?" he nodded.

Marianne could still hear the screaming, she had wanted Wes to go back to sleep and spare him the sounds she was hearing. She ran back downstairs. It had been fifteen minutes and the cops had not arrived yet. Now she heard the young man being struck and thrown around. She peeked out the peephole and could hear him begging. "NO! PLEASE STOP! NO!" Over and over again he was struck and thrown about. She sunk down by the door, crying she prayed aloud, "Dear lord…please help him. Tell me what I should do? Should I try to help him? Should I open the door? I'm so scared! Don't let him die lord, please don't let him die!" She felt torn, her job was to protect the children. What if she helped and the attacker got inside? Then what? Would they kill her and the children too for being witnesses? She wanted to open the door and help him, but she knew pitifully that she couldn't, it would be too risky.

Marianne called 911 again. "Hello 911 wha-" She interrupted, "Where are the cops? I have been waiting twenty-five minutes for them to save this man who is being killed!" "I am sorry, we sent them. They will be there soon." Marianne hung up angrily.

She listened to every single scream, every single blow, every single cry, and she cried with him, the young man who was being murdered right outside the Colburn's apartment. She cried and cried and prayed continuously swaying back and forth like a child, sometimes covering her ears. "Please, God…don't let him die. Let the cops get here in time. Please…please…please!" After forty-five minutes the screaming stopped. Her eyes were swollen from the crying and her nose was running everywhere, her hair a disheveled mess. She looked at the door on her knees, she put her ear against it and listened. She heard nothing.

Marianne laid back down on the sofa and cried herself to sleep. The next morning the children woke her up with the sounds of cartoons. "Good morning Marianne!" they were hopping and eating cereal out of the box. She sat up quickly and looked out the peephole. There was blood everywhere. "You two stay here. I'll be right back." She slipped on her shoes and opened the door. Blood was all over the concrete and the other apartment doors. The police had put up yellow tape and cones. There was a massive amount of blood in the parking lot. Enough to cover almost two parking spaces. She felt sick.

She waved down a young officer. "What happened last night? Why didn't the police ever come? I called 911 twice. I listened to this last night! Did you find him?" The young officer replied with little emotion, "We found the body of nineteen-year-old Claudio Trinidad. We don't know who did this, but this is a really bad neighborhood. I imagine the officers on duty, thought it was drug related and didn't want to get involved."

"So, that's it? He was beaten to death last night by someone who was enjoying it. It took them forty-five minutes to kill him, and they listened to him scream and beg for mercy for the entire time!" The young cop nodded nonchalantly, "You can leave a statement, if you'd like." Marianne walked back inside and grabbed towels and cleaned the blood off the Colburns door, hoping the children would never see it.

She heard her phone ring and picked it up, "Hi Marianne! Good morning. How did last night go? Jake and I are just grabbing breakfast. We're bringing home donuts for you and the children." Marianne stayed quiet for a moment not knowing what to say, "Mrs. Colburn, I'm washing blood off your front door. There was a murder last night…"

# Haunted

Robby liked the house they lived in before better, but it wasn't up to him. It was up to his parents. So, they moved from the city of Lilburn, Georgia to the city of Lawrenceville, Georgia when he was twelve years old. From a perfectly flat level driveway (perfect for riding his bike at least) to one of those way too-creepy vertical ones. He could never quite manage getting the courage to ride his bike all the way down from the top. He could only do it from halfway down. Outside during the day everything felt normal. The neighbors were friendly, his school was nice, there was even a few stray cats that would come around and play for a bit, but inside the house something was wrong.

The old house was kinda ugly on the outside, until spring came around and azaleas would make it look pretty. The Lawrenceville house had not a single tree or shrub. It was three stories and ugly all year long. The backyard was huge but for some reason Robby and his brother Sean never played in it. It just didn't feel right for some reason. They lived there Robby, and Sean along with their mom and dad. On the inside it was nice enough. It wasn't haunted in the traditional way, maybe it was just cursed. Maybe there was a dead body in the back yard or maybe a native American cursed the grounds centuries ago. Or maybe it had been involved in the civil war, who knew? It doesn't matter why it was spiritually dirty, but somehow it was, and bad things happened there.

One day while everyone was sitting down in the living room actually laughing and having fun, one of their mother's huge heavy paintings with a glass frame that had been hanging over the staircase simply fell and crashed, shattering to the ground for no reason. Their mom had been a professional framer at one point and knew how to hang a painting properly. It had hung there for a year and a half but on that day it just fell all by itself. It was lucky it hadn't fallen on someone coming down the stairs or they would have had to go to the ER.

There were certain things they all knew about the Lawrenceville house but never spoke about, such as the downstairs, the lowest level. It had a large den, a spare bedroom, and the laundry room. There were five windows down there but no matter what time of day it was, or what season it was, it was always freezing. No house in Georgia had any business being that cold in the middle of summer, but it was ice cold all year long.

One-night Robby heard soft pretty bells that seemed to travel past the main bedrooms on the top level where they all slept. Up and down the hall the bells rang, but Robby ignored it and went to back to sleep. Another night Sean woke him up, "Robby, wake up. My bed is shaking, and I hear scratching at my window. Robby woke up, yawned, and felt complete surprise. Sean was not the fearful type. It was Robby who had wet the bed out of fear of the dark sometimes, not Sean. Robby had asked Sean if he could sleep with him multiple time throughout their childhood. Sean was the reliable one, the dependable one. So, Sean waking him up like this felt backwards.

The boys walked into Sean's bedroom and saw the bed was shaking. They heard the sound of scratching at the window, yet the window was on the third story, and there were no trees, no branches in sight. "Let's pray." The two Catholic boys looked at each other, held hands and said the 'Lord's Prayer' aloud and then followed it with the 'Hail Mary'. The bed stopped shaking and the scratching stopped. "Are you okay?" Robby asked Sean. Sean nodded, "Yeah, it's happened before, but I just pray, and it goes away. The scratching sound that was worse and that was new. I think I'm gonna sleep in the spare room downstairs tonight." Robby was shocked, "Downstairs? You're crazy!" Sean grabbed his pillow sleepily, "I'll be fine. It's better than this room." Robby persisted, "But it's freezing down there. You know that!" Sean waved him away as if pushing his words back, "I'll be fine…stop worrying. Go back to bed now."

The next morning Robby overheard Sean telling their mother about something that happened to him that night, in the downstairs bedroom. He shamelessly eavesdropped on their conversation, "Something pulled at the sheets, and held me down. It whispered nasty things to me. I couldn't move! It held me down and snarled. It molested me mom…for like thirty minutes! I want us to leave this house." He heard his mom's voice react, "We can't honey. The rent here is affordable, and we are in a contract. I'm sorry that happened to you. Sleep in your brother's room next time you get scared. Okay?" Sean stayed quiet and nodded.

Robby felt bad for him. It was as if the house was picking on him in particular. Robby noticed Sean was sick more in that house, he had several infections and missed weeks of school. He had never been sickly before just while they lived in that particular house.

But it was as if the house had a sense of humor or perhaps a sense of balance because it got their mother next. She had been doing laundry that night and had to go downstairs to do it. It was dark and the only lights she used were the laundry room lights which was literally a single hanging bulb. Suddenly she heard laughing in the den, the largest room downstairs, past the laundry room at the end of the long hallway. She felt chills, Robby and Sean were playing with their friends two blocks away. Their father was still at work. No one should be laughing in the den right now. The laughter sounded like a recording on an old toy, distorted, male and sinister. For some reason it reminded her of a clown toy. What else could be laughing by itself? She looked around in the spare bedroom closet for anything electronic, perhaps a walkie talkie could be making the sound, she thought. She then checked the few boxes in the laundry room as well, just in case, but the laughing continued, and it seemed to be coming from different directions now moving around from room to room. Finally, she peeked inside the oversized dark den from where she had first heard the laughing coming from but had mentally tried to avoid admitting it to herself. Was there a man there? A stranger? No, but what she did see there in the far-left corner of the room was a pair of slightly larger than human glowing red eyes on something that was about four and a half feet tall, standing alone in the corner. Their mom had perfect eyesight back then, she knew exactly what she saw. She stared at it for a few minutes, the eyes seemed to be smiling yet exuded pure evil as well. She ran up the stairs and heard it follow her, it spoke, "I know what you want…I know what you want…hahaha…Run, oh no, don't run! Hahaha…don't run up those stairs! Weren't you just looking for me?" She felt it behind her, mocking her, she could feel it's warmth on her heels, hear it stomping up the stairs with her, she knew instinctively it had to stay down there. If she could just get to the top of the stairs it would stop chasing her. She raced up and ran past the kitchen to the living room, the least scary room in the house. There she waited alone, until the boys and her husband came back home, then she finally felt safe again.

Their father had not gone untouched by whatever lingered in those walls. He had always been strict but at the Lawrenceville house he was especially angry. He had thrown things in violent rages, had broken nice objects he had once prized, and was even more calloused and rough on the boys. Sean was the older brother at fifteen years old. One night he threatened to call the police if their father hurt him again, and their dad had gotten on top of him and straddled him. They were in the downstairs den, and the yelling had woken up Robby. Their father was holding Sean down while Sean cried and tried to wriggle away for an hour. Their father was just laughing at him, at his pain. A few months later Sean turned sixteen, got a job, bought a car, and moved out. Robby envied him his freedom. They left the house too that year.

Years later Robby told a girlfriend about the house, they drove to it at her request. Looking at the dark windows she asked, "Which one was your brother's window? Wow, there are still no trees here!" Robby laughed, "Um…it was that one!" at that exact moment the lights of that single window came on. The couple jumped out of their seats laughing and drove away.

# Something happened there...
### based on a true story

\* *As a side note for my readers. For some reason while I was typing this story, strange things kept happening with the fonts and words during this story specifically. Even the title seemed to distort itself on the screen, when I asked others around me, they could see it too. The photo above is the actual house, I want it to be a film titled, 'Something happened there...'*

# Triangle

Xiomara was a striking nineteen-year-old Latina. She had two jobs; one as a barista at a local European style café and one as a cocktail waitress at a nightclub. Her handsome Italian Irish boyfriend Tom was in college learning computer animation at the local Art Institute nearby. They shared a cozy one-bedroom apartment in the city and were madly happily in love. They painted together, sang together, and were the type of couple that made others jealous or nauseous.

Every day Tom would look into Xiomara's eyes and tell her she was the most beautiful girl in the world, and he really meant it. Xiomara tried to spoil Tom as well, with regular little surprises and gifts. Their pet names for each other were Marc Antony and Cleopatra.

Everything was almost perfect except Xiomara's ability to see, hear and feel things no one else could. She was overwhelmed with psychic ability that she did not want and could not control. On top of all that she was a sleepwalker and had an unexplainable fear of the moon. They couldn't go anywhere without her having an "experience" of some sort.

One time it was at a party when the ghost of a young man named Todd, had wanted to talk to another person there and apologize for committing suicide. Other times it was a terribly horrible dream or vision that would upset and embarrass Tom, because she would tell others around them such as their friends and family. But once her predictions came true, he would forgive her, but still the messages began to take their toll on him.

Xiomara kept a moon journal in which she tracked her bad dream and sleepwalking incidents to certain lunar activities. She loved science and had ideas for a time travel machine and had detailed theories about the nature of the universe. In one moment, she seemed brilliant in another she would be screaming over a cockroach in fear. Her unpredictability was part of why he loved her so much and also why Tom sometimes felt disconnected from her.

When she slept walk she would scream, "No! No! No!" and walk around in circles, or sometimes she would sway back and forth on the floor then abruptly come back to bed. Other nights she would remove her cloths and start organizing objects in non-sensical ways, she would wake up with piles of stuff at her feet.

One month she told him she saw moving stars. "Don't you see them?" She pointed to the night sky. "They're moving around everywhere, almost dancing!" At that point he really began to worry that maybe she was schizophrenic or something.

Her nightmares got worse and worse. "I'm slipping out of my body Tom. They aren't just dreams anymore. I go to different worlds.

Courtney says it's 'astral projection." Courtney was one of her weirdo friends that claimed to be able to see angels and demons everywhere. "I'm scared Tom. Sometimes I go to scary places with black and white clowns. They have their own world, complete with strange TV shows and everything. I can't come back. Courtney says that's not normal. When a person astral projects it supposed to be perfectly safe. They can't get hurt and they are supposed to snap back into their body the second they think about being back in bed. But that's not happening to me…I'm gone longer and longer each time it happens and no matter how much I want to come back to my body I can't! Last night, I got stuck in this world that looked like white noise, like from a channel on a television. I was just wandering alone in static for what seemed like hours and hours."

When she first started "flying around" as Tom called it, she saw beautiful bright happy places.

Then her astral trips became progressively worse and worse. One night she woke him up with her hyperventilating. She was asleep, but her body was taking huge massive breaths over and over again, her chest rising high repeatedly. He called her name and gently shook her, trying to wake her up. Finally, after about five minutes she took her last exaggerated breath and woke up terrified. "I was being attacked! It was beating me up and trying to kill me! It told me I wasn't allowed to heal people and learn about energy anymore! It kept hurting me! It was wearing a black pointy witch hat and every time I tried to fly away it would snatch me back and hurt me! I couldn't see its face, but it had a scary raspy old lady voice!" she cried in his arms. Tom felt utterly useless.

It got to the point where she would astral project almost every night. "Tom, I don't fly anymore. When it happens now, I am locked in my body and I can feel something watching over us, in the room. I see an alien now; he's trying to get me to accept his friendship. He told me he will give me powers to see the future and make me famous if I accept him. He showed me a future with all these things I could do if I said yes to him. But he was so ugly and disgusting to me. I said no. I felt so repulsed by him. He could hear my thoughts and read my mind. That alien is mad at me Tom, I offended him…he has a huge spaceship Tom, as big as our sky!" she cried, "When will it stop? I just want it all to go away. I just want to be normal. Make it go away, please Tom. Please, I can't take it anymore…I feel like I'm going crazy."

Tom gave her some homeopathic sleeping pills, she drifted back to sleep. He went and sat down in the living room. He asked aloud that night while sitting there, "Leave her alone. Whatever is wrong with her, whatever she has…this gift? Take it away from her and give it to me. I can handle it.

Give me the visons, the dreams, the astral projection. Give me her burden! Give it to me!" he looked up to god and around himself, hoping his plea had been heard.

A week later Xiomara stopped sleep walking and couldn't hear ghosts anymore. She had slept fine all week long and had hope again. She couldn't wait to tell Tom about it, he was on his way home from a night class. She stepped out onto the terrace and waved down to him, smiling a radiant sincere smile. She couldn't remember the last time she felt so free.

Tom heard a voice as he approached the sidewalk, "Stop. Wait here a second." it said. "What?" he swung around, "Who said that?" he was alone. Just then, a speeding truck drove right past him so close he almost fell backwards. He was shocked. The voice had saved his life. He blew it off and got closer to his building, he saw Xiomara smiling at him from the high terrace. He blew her a kiss and she mimed catching it in her hand, placed it on her lips and blew one back at him.

Tom heard the voice again. "Look up now." There above his building was a massive black triangular UFO hovering silently, directly over his building it had a few lights around it and one large red glowing circle in the middle. "Yeah, I'm not seeing that…" he mumbled looking down. He chose to ignore it completely, and calmly walked upstairs to greet his lovely happy girlfriend.

*This is what the UFO looked like.*

# Blackout

Imagine waking up in a strange place with strange people hovering over you, and you have no idea how you got there. Now imagine that happening often. Scary, right?

That was Gabriel Speed's life. The first time it happened in a public restroom when he was a teenager. He didn't remember going to the bathroom but when he woke up, twenty people were looking down on him, asking him if he was okay. He worried, worried about being mugged or that maybe someone had drugged him, or hit him on the head, but it didn't happen again until a few years later.

He had graduated college and was working in the city as an account executive for a tire company. A group of old buddies, some from college, and some from high school had all called him on the same day. He had the brilliant idea of telling them all to meet him at the same local pub. He was the first to arrive and ordered a Guinness beer while he waited for his pals to get there. He was staring at the foam at the top of his pint glass and that's when he noticed it, he caught it for the first time *the cloaking*. He had not even had a sip of his beer when all of the sudden he felt a big heavy black cloak come around from in back of him, swing over his right shoulder and cover his face, and that was it. Lights out for Gabriel.

The next morning, he was in his condo bed with no clue as to how he got there. Three of his buddies were there. One of them named Mike, was frying eggs, and burning toast. Jonathan and Syd were playing video games.

Gabriel felt weak and stumbled into his living room, "What happened last night?"

Mike asked, "Hey Gabe. You want some eggs?" Gabriel tried again, "No. I want to know what happened last night? I don't remember anything."

Mike answered him, "What do you mean what happened? We all went bar hopping. We played a game of darts and pool. One of your friends left because he hooked up with a girl. We danced a bit at the last place. How can you not remember? You didn't even drink that much. In fact, I don't remember you even finishing your beer from the pub." Gabriel shrugged, "I don't know...I just don't. It's weird. I guess, I should just be glad I made it home in one piece."

Jonathan was half ass listening to the conversation and offered his two cents, "Well, I took a bunch of pics and posted them. Go look in my phone Gabe. Maybe something in there will jog your memory" Gabriel grabbed his friend's phone and saw himself laughing and making faces. It scared him. *That wasn't me...I didn't do any of those things last night.* There were pictures of him on the dance floor. Pictures of him looking serious in a group photo, and another of him winking and making a jackass of himself. Gabriel didn't recognize the look in his eyes. It was someone else entirely. "How was I acting? Was I acting normal?"

They all chimed in that yes he had made jokes, laughed a lot, and even flirted with a few women. Syd suggested, "Hey maybe you should check your phone too. I think you got a few new numbers; you were talking to one girl for like an hour." Gabriel jumped up and looked for his phone. He went to his bedroom surprised to find it on its charger exactly where it was supposed to be. He was impressed with his split personality for doing that. He flipped through his notifications and saw he had new text messages. The first one read:

> hi this is Beverly

Followed by a second text:

> i really want to see you again. had fun last night

The second one came with a pic of her. She had long dark hair and wore lots of makeup. She had a small scar on her lower lip. She looked a bit sweaty from clubbing, but she was a 7 out of 10 otherwise.

Gabriel was a bit intrigued and texted back:

You free tomorrow for dinner?

A few minutes passed, and her reply was:

Yes? How about Wisteria that new restaurant? 7:00?

He didn't waste any time and immediately replied:

Sure! Sounds good. See you then!

Gabriel walked back into the living room, "I have a date!" He felt a pillow hit his face just then and had no idea who threw it. Syd remarked, "Gee, I hope you remember it! You want me to call you tomorrow and remind you?" They laughed at him, "Yeah, maybe you should tie a bow on your finger!" added another, "And write her name on your hand!" He faked laughing along with them, but he scratched his head and thought...*Maybe I should.*

The next night he got ready for his date and headed out. He arrived at the restaurant exactly at 7:00 and she was there waiting for him at the bar. They had a good time. Beverly was interesting, funny, and sexy. She was a painter, an artist and was known for her realistic murals. The only bump in their conversation was when Gabriel mentioned her scar and asked how she got it. In that moment her eyes twitched, and she stuttered a bit, shifted in her seat. Stammering so much he felt uncomfortable and regretted asking her. Finally, she simply admitted she'd rather not talk about it. The restaurant had a dance floor and they danced for a few songs. The music was sensual and slow. He held her body close and she pressed up against him. There was electricity between them, and it felt good. She suggested going back to her studio, so she could show him some of her work. That sounded like a lot of fun to him, so he paid the bill and took some cash out of his wallet to leave a tip for their server.

Beverly put on her jacket when she noticed a friend of hers at the bar, "Oh that's my girlfriend. Hold on just a sec, let me say a quick "hi" to her. I'll be right back!" He watched her talking and was feeling so excited. Anxious to kiss her finally and discover more of her body... *Of course she would have to see one of her stupid girlfriends right now just before we leave. So annoying!* He thought to himself as he stood there waiting for her. She waved at him and he waved back smiling, trying to look like a nice patient guy and not like the annoyed horny guy. She was just about to walk away, she was giving her friend a goodbye hug and kiss. *Yes! We're leaving...* He thought and then it happened again. He felt the dark heavy black cloak coming over his head...*No! Not again. Not now! Can't anyone else see this? No*...But it was too late. Lights out for Gabriel again.

When he came to, he was hanging fifty feet, on top of an old electrical transmission tower it was still night time. Gabriel had a profound fear of heights. "What the hell? Where am I?" he looked down and started crying. The tower was in a field behind an old apartment building that looked like it should be condemned. The wind was blowing him around, normally he liked wind very much but now it just seemed cruel.

"Stay calm Gabe. Stay calm. Don't look down...just don't look down. Uh...God how did I get here? I was on a date, we were about to go to her place and make out! How the hell?" The situation reminded him of werewolf movies in which the lycanthrope wakes up in a strange place the next day naked. "At least I'm not naked." He accidently looked down. "Never mind, I'd rather be on the ground butt ass naked!" He had slippery dress shoes on and standing on the steel and hanging was not easy. He slowly began to climb down. He had gotten down about 35 feet and figured he had about 15 feet more to go. His muscles ached, hands were blistered and sweaty. He was tired and the vertigo he felt made everything seem so confusing. He felt the cloak coming again but this time he tried to fight it by shaking his head vigorously but then he felt inexplicable fears from his childhood invade his mind. Out of nowhere he felt worried about his little sister...*Kerri, I have to find Kerri she's lost out there...in those buildings...those old buildings. The bullies from school they're going to hurt her. Don't worry Kerri! I'm coming! I'll save you!*

He looked down and the ground didn't seem so far away anymore, he felt rushed like he had to jump and find Kerri quickly. He let go and for some strange reason he thought he heard Beverly screaming at him from close by, "Gabriel, no don't let go!" but it was too late he felt himself falling through the steel structure. His bones cracked, and clothes tore, skin cutting as he hit so many metal beams of the tower along the way down. He hit the ground hard. The damn cloak came over his head again.

He woke up next in an ambulance, a police officer was yelling at him, "Calm down sir. Or, I'll arrest you!" He had no idea what he had been doing before that minute of lucidity, but he leaned back and tried to be calm. *Who found me?* He wondered...*Who called the ambulance? Was it Beverly? Had she been there the whole time?* Again, he felt the cloaking, as they took Gabriel to the hospital.

He woke up in a hospital bed. He saw his destroyed cloths and terrible bumps, deep purple bruises, and cuts on his body from head to toe. The only thing that didn't hurt was his face miraculously. But the sides and back of his head did. He wanted to see Beverly and find out what happened. He needed answers or at least clues. He got out of bed and the nurses insisted he not wander around yet and to lay back down. He saw them put a sedative in his IV line and once again his lights were out.

That morning he woke up in the same hospital bed, he felt relieved to be safe at least. He didn't have his phone on him. The first thing he desperately wanted to do was talk to Beverly, but he did not have his phone. Luckily, he remembered her last name and used the phone in his room to get information and call her. She picked up, "Hello?"

"Beverly? It's me Gabriel. What happened last night? I'm in the hospital now do-" She interrupted him, "You know what creep? I don't know what you did! You left with some other girl from the restaurant! It was totally embarrassing! I had just finished telling my friend how much I like you and then you just walked out with someone else. Now you call me with this bullshit? Whatever Gabriel. Do not call me ever again!"

"Wait! Please don-" *Hang up...* he thought. Gabriel felt disheartened. His phone was missing, and his wallet was missing. The strange thing was he apparently left it at Wisteria, the restaurant he went to with Beverly. No one had stolen anything; he had just left them there intact.

Gabriel never found out what happened that night and even though he tried Beverly wouldn't give him any extra details and refused to have anything to do with him. He came home that day looking like he had been beaten up. He didn't know what the cloak was, was it another personality? Was he crazy? Was it some kind of demon? He obsessed over it for months feeling scared to do anything outside his home. Gabriel became nonsocial and a bit of a hermit. He became scared of the dark, like a child. He had so many questions no one he knew could answer, and this made it seem like a part of him would always be stuck under the cloak.

Years later Gabriel walked by a store window and happened to see a painting of a man hanging from a tower. The details were uncanny. There was an old building in it and the man looked exactly like him. He felt confused and shocked. He looked for the artist signature and saw, "Beverly Warner" neatly painted in the corner.

# Total Darkness

It was October of course; this is a scary story! But no, seriously it really was October. The leaves were afire, and clouds seemed thicker with puffy heavy grayness. Children were stoked about their costumes, their future candy earnings, and the scariest stories they could get their little brains on!

*In the principal's office, Hopkins Elementary School*

Mrs. Brown had sent for Jennifer Essex, and Heather Hall. The two little girls had been suspected of vandalizing the girls' restroom. Mrs. Brown was annoyed, she brought her lunch of BBQ chicken and coleslaw in her office and ate it, as she interrogated the girls. She was hungry, and she did not care if the students had to watch her cut up her meat and discipline them at the same time.

"So, which of you wants to tell me what happened? Hmm? In the girls' bathroom?" she took a large bite of chicken and chewed with as much grace as possible. The two girls looked at each other. Heather stayed quiet. It was Jennifer, the fastest girl in the school that spoke up, "I'll tell you but you're not gonna believe us…" Jennifer looked over at her accomplice who was shaking her head as if to say, "No, don't tell her".

Jennifer explained to the other little girl, "If we don't, we'll get in trouble." Mrs. Brown said in all seriousness before shoving a bite of coleslaw in her mouth, "Oh, you are both in trouble either way, so you might as well fess up ladies."

Jennifer offered this **tiny bit of information**, "We were only playing a game. It wasn't us."

*A few days earlier, Hopkins Elementary School*

In the cafeteria that marvelous fall afternoon at Hopkins Elementary school was a group of third grade girls telling each other urban legends at lunchtime. Someone brought up the game 'Bloody

Mary' and that's when things got really heated. There was a massive debate on how to do it properly. A blonde girl with pigtails and yellow ribbons in her hair spoke with authority, "You have to say it in a dark room. No lights, and then you call her name." "Well, what happens?" asked little Paige. "You see her face in the mirror and she reaches out to grab you!" answered little chubby Tina with pink plastic glasses. "No, no, no! You are all wrong!" announced little Nichole. "You do have do it in a place with no light at all. Like a bathroom, or a closet. And you have to have a mirror too! Then you look into the mirror say Bloody Mary nine times and on the tenth time you say, "Bloody Mary, I've got your baby!" That's why she comes, because she wants her baby back!"

They all got chills. "Well…" asked the little tomboy one Jennifer, "Have you ever done it?"

Some of them acted like they had but in reality none of them had tried it.

Jennifer and Heather were best friends forever. They looked at each other and smiled mischievously. "Let's do it! If one of us holds the switch down there's no light at all in the bathroom. Let's do it before we go back to class!" the other girls were supportive, "Tell us what happens!" they demanded, "Yeah, tell us if you see her face!". Soon the bell rang, and the two eight-year-old girls snuck off to the restroom together. They giggled and whispered with glee, completely stupidly fearless.

They entered into the bathroom, luckily they were alone. Heather offered to hold the light switch down, it was the type that needed weight on it to stay on the off position and Jennifer, the slightly more curious one stood in front of the center mirror. There were three sinks and each one had a very large square mirror above it.

Jennifer looked at Heather, "Okay, ready?" Heather nodded enthusiastically, "Ready, but I'm kinda scared now!" she laughed. Jennifer ordered, "Now. Get the lights."

They saw absolutely nothing. The restroom had no windows and the door was too far away for the cracks of light to illuminate anything. Jennifer began, "Bloody Mary. Bloody Mary. Bloody Mary. Bloody Mary…" she felt something then, a presence around her like a smoky snake around her feet and moving behind her, but she didn't let it spook her. She continued, "Bloody Mary. Bloody Mary. Bloody Mary…" then when she got to the tenth one she switched to, "Bloody Mary I've got your baby." She did see something white in the mirror for a quick spark, it was like a plain looking pilgrim woman's face. Heather couldn't take it and the lights came back on.

"What happened?" Jennifer scolded her friend. Heather shrugged, "I got too scared. I'm going back to class now, okay?" then she walked out.

Jennifer looked back at the mirrors and was stunned. She saw all three huge mirrors had been broken. In each one was now a perfect 'M', cracked perfectly into the glass. Each 'M' was a capital but a slightly different 'M'. The arch was wide on one and long on another. She reached out and touched the mirror in front of her. "How did that happen?" she asked aloud. A person couldn't crack glass like that with such precision without causing other cracks, not in just a few seconds at least, she concluded.

Bloody Mary had come. Jennifer walked out of the girl's restroom backwards not wanting to take her eyes off the mirrors.

When she got back to class she told the other girls what happened. It was legendary. All the girls went to see it. Eventually that bathroom became known as the 'Bloody Mary Bathroom'.

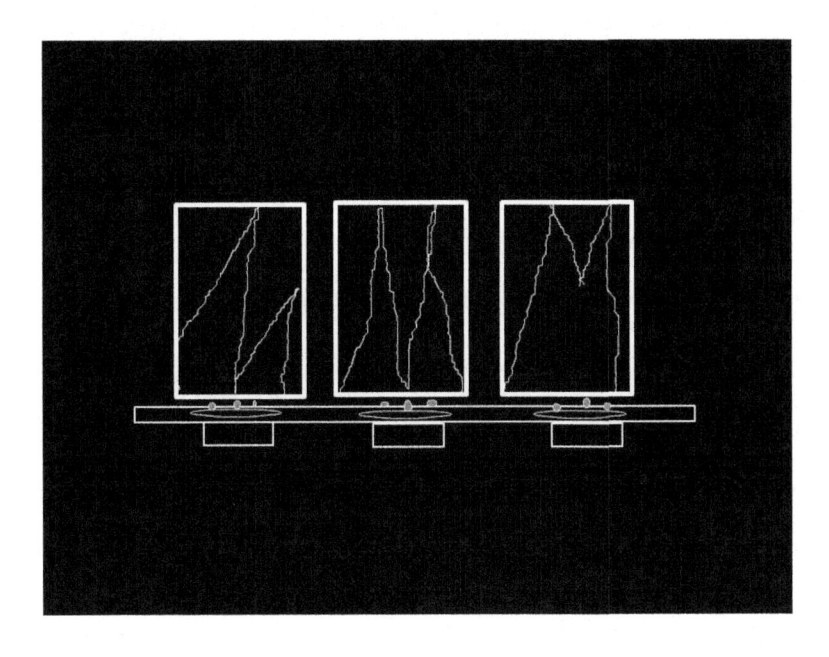

*This is what the mirror M's looked like.*

# The Devil's Number

It was the early 1990's when traditional phone landlines were still a thing and smart phones didn't exist yet. Most people still had land lines and only the very tech savvy had cell phones back then. It was Heidy's birthday party, a slumber party to be exact. She was in the 5th grade. Earlier they had all eaten cake, opened presents, eaten pizza and watched scary movies. Her parents went to bed after the presents and left the girls in the lower half of the split-level floor. There were sleeping bags of all different shades of soft pastels sprawled about the carpet along with dolls, pillows, and stuffed animals everywhere. It had been a pure sugar and spice kind of night.

But there is always bad seed among the good fruit. That night the bad seed was Missy. Missy was mean and the 5th grade bully. She was Italian, short, and smart. She was easily the tiniest one, but her personality was so dominant she had become a master at getting the other girls to do her bidding.

In the past she had made several girls at school cry with her hurtful taunting or mean truth or dare games. This night she had something special in mind. "So, have you ever called the devil?" They all murmured different answers, but all seem confused by the very question. "What do you mean Missy? Like out loud? Why would anyone want to talk to him?" Some girls turned their noses up showing their agreement.

Missy laughed, "No, not out loud dummy! On his phone of course. He has a phone number you know?" She started laughing manically. "It's 666-6666!" Some of them laughed with her. Heidy, the glowing birthday girl asked, "Are you joking around or being serious? I can't tell, you are always acting crazy!" she slapped Missy on her lap to get her attention and in an attempt to get her to stop laughing so hard.

Missy struggled to catch her breath, "No, no, no! It's real I'm serious! Grab the cordless phone! Someone hand me the cordless!" One by one in a single file chain they passed down the cordless until Missy had it in her tiny strong hand. She announced, "Shhhhh!!! I'm going to call him now. Everyone shut up and listen!"

Complete silence was cast about the room like a blanket. Missy dialed 666-6666 so they all could see; they were all huddled close to her now listening.

The phone rang once, twice, and then a third time. "Just hang up. It's not a real number." Murmured one impatient partygoer. Just then the ringing stopped, and someone picked up.

There was a collective gasp in the room. At first there was a long silence but then a song started playing. It was so eerie and strange. It was fast paced and repetitive. It played over and over again.

Missy smiled; all the girls listened with their jaws dropped.

The music stopped abruptly, and the Devil hung up. There were a few seconds of the girls looking around and then they all collectively chimed in with squeals, oohs and ahhs.

Missy looked proud of herself and yelled, "I told you so! And you all thought I was making it up!" One or two Christian girls started praying and crying, holding hands they decided they wanted nothing to do with Missy's voodoo, and pulled their sleeping bags away from the group. Heidy apologized to them and offered to let them sleep in her bedroom with the lights on. They took her up on her offer and left with their pillows and blankets to the safety of Heidy's upstairs lavender rose-colored bedroom, complete with a white princess style canopy bed.

Missy stuck her tongue out at them as they passed her, "Bunch a cry babies…" she snickered.

She was still holding the phone when it rang. Missy jumped out of her skin. The phone slipped away. Heidy picked it up and answered, "Hello?" On the other end all she could hear was strange electronic sounds. Almost like robotic talking. It stopped, then hung up. "Oh my god, Heidy who was it?" the girls asked.

"I don't know I couldn't understand it." Lorie a blonde girl with a bad perm yet very pretty face suggested, "Maybe, it was him! The Devil, he called us back!"

The phone rang again. They all jumped and huddled. Heidy confessed "I'm not picking it up." Missy picked it up and answered, "Hello?" this time the voice was less electronic and easier to understand, "You let me in, now I'm inside." said the voice on the other end. Missy actually started crying. Which shocked everyone because Missy never ever cries. "Oh my God…it's a monster." she shrieked, and the lights switched off.

The girls screamed! Heidy reached for the light switch and pushed it back up. "Is everyone okay?" The girls gave mixed messages some were truly scared, and some were having a blast. "How did that happen? Did someone mess around and flip the light switch off" Heidy asked the group of girls. They all nodded no, and pinky swore their complete innocence. It had been five minutes and the phone rang again. This time no one answered it. Heidy's older brother Eric came down the stairs in his flannel pajamas and asked, "Which one of you is Missy?" Missy looked worried, "I am." She raised her hand as if in school. Eric handed her his red cordless phone, "Here, it's your dad." and went back upstairs.

Missy spoke into the phone, "Hello daddy?" on the other end she heard a masculine, yet distorted voice say, "Missy." And then the strange song from before played. The Devil's song played over and over again. She dropped the phone and held herself, "It's not my dad. It's him again."

Anita, a skeptical girl with a retainer in her mouth picked up the phone and listened, she hung it up, "It was nothing. Just the operator."

Heidy sweetly suggested, "Why don't we all go to sleep now? No more scary stuff!" They all brushed their teeth and Heidy turned out the lights.

It wasn't but five minutes later and the phone rang again, Missy screamed, "Put the lights on! Somebody please put the lights on!" no one picked up the phone this time. Missy kept going, "I saw a glowing smile and eyes it was moving side to side over there by the windows! It looked like a mean smiley clown face. It was wearing a black hood! Didn't anyone else see it?"

The girls looked and saw nothing. Heidy calmed her down and was able to turn out the lights but three minutes later Missy screamed again. She was the only one who was being tormented, she kept hearing the phone ring when it wasn't or at least no one else was hearing it the times she was.

The thing in the window appeared every time the lights were turned off, but she was the only one who could see it. Heidy compromised with Missy by leaving the laundry room light on, which was next to the party room, it was enough light to keep Missy calm yet dark enough for the other girls to fall asleep.

Missy was never the same again she felt constantly haunted by ghosts and bad spirits. She was in a terrible car accident soon afterwards in which she broke both her legs, and her mother suffered a near fatal head injury. Her mother's best friend who was driving the car was killed instantly. The ghost of her mother's friend would appear to Missy throughout her life even in adulthood, tormenting her with her unexpected presence.

Sometimes even simple paintings upset her and things that should not move seemed to come alive but only for her.

*A side note for my readers. I am not sure how it will translate in e-book format but in my writing file this book by complete "coincidence" landed on page number 66. I was unnerved by this. Heidy is a real person, and all the terrible things did happen sadly. When writing this, the document indented its own paragraphs and I could not change it, that has never happened before it was almost as if it was writing itself, it pressed enter for me...until I finished typing it out.*

# Fukushima: Daiichi Nuclear Catastrophe Update

Stephanie Wolfe

Our society desperately needs to reexamine the Fukushima, Daiichi nuclear catastrophe. What exactly happened? Is it safer now? How does it compare to Chernobyl, is it the same or far worse? What are the Japanese doing to fix it, or is it unfixable? What has it done to our planet? Our animals, people, and environment? These are incredibly important questions. The answers are terrifying. The answers point for the need to ban nuclear energy worldwide. International action must be taken, to safeguard the planet from anymore nuclear damage. Sadly, the best, most capable human minds have caused the most damage to our planet. Maybe human intelligence is actually a curse.

On March 11, 2011 Japan was struck with a 9.0 earthquake at 2:46 pm; causing a deadly 49.2-foot tsunami (Death toll about 19,000) that "disabled the power supply and cooling of three Fukushima Daiichi reactors," (World Nuclear Association). The three cores melted by March 14, 2011. Because of the radiation, standard emergency assistance was impossible to enforce. On March 15, in unit 2 there was a hydrogen explosion, the largest source of radioactive release from this particular nuclear disaster.

"Had I known that the Germans would not succeed in producing an atomic bomb, I would have never lifted a finger." (Albert Einstein, in his letter to Roosevelt)

Fukushima is one of the largest of Japan's 47 prefectures, it lies just 93 miles from the Pacific shores in the mountains of Honshu. "The no-entry zone around the nuclear plant makes up less than 3% of its area, while the rest is safe for tourists to visit." according to the Japanese tourism guide website

"At 1.24 am on 26 April 1986 Chernobyl's Unit 4 reactor exploded after staff disabled safety systems and performed an ill-advised experiment to check – ironically enough – the reactor's safety." (Mark Lynas) So, how does the Fukushima disaster compare to Chernobyl? Both are rated a maximum level-7 by the International Nuclear and Radiological Event Scale (INES) scale. Chris Busby, a professor (University of Ulster) assessed after a visit to Japan, "Fukushima is still boiling its radionuclides all over Japan. Chernobyl went up in one go. So, Fukushima is worse." It's been seven years since the core meltdown. Tepco, (Tokyo Electric Power Company) and the reactor employees have done incredible work. Japan sends regular copies of their updated reports on radiation in the ground, seawater, and the Daiichi Nuclear Power Station.

"People can foresee the future only when it coincides with their own wishes, and the most grossly obvious facts can be ignored when they are unwelcome." (George Orwell)

In April 2018, they released a hazard map to reporters. The map shows green zones that are now safe enough to walk around with light clothes and masks. But Tepco must continue to pour water over the melted nuclear fuel. One of the growing challenges they face is how to dispose of the all the stored contaminated water. The Nuclear Regulation Authority has given Japan permission to dump the water into the sea after first having it diluted and filtered. Tepco, intends to hold onto the water until 2021. Japan fears public backlash from fishermen, who were hit tremendously with international regulations. They have just recently begun to sell Tilapia to Thailand again, since it tested normal. Japan believes the longer they hold onto the water, the more likely the public will forget about the whole incident. But beautiful nearby cities, Tomioka, once treasured for its lovely delicate cherry blossoms have had evacuation status lifted, yet their populations will most likely never be restored. The residents do not want to move back, for fear of radiation.

"Is there anything more frightening than people?" (Svetlana Alexievich, Chernobyl witness)

As far as they have come and as hard as they have worked, Tepco believes it will ultimately take another 30 to 40 years to deactivate and finally shut down the plant. Luckily, evacuations were fast and there were few human deaths as a direct result to the melt down. (There were deaths among the employees that were the first to cool down the cores.)

Animal life directly near the reactors location did cease. Most studies have been dedicated to sea life in the nearby ecosystems, such as mollusks, crustaceans, who after being tested have proven to be quite resilient to radiation. It is thought to be because of the ion-rich environment. One researcher Dr. Shin-ichi Hayama, veterinarian; who happened to be studying Japanese macaques monkeys in Fukushima since 2008, noticed three main changes after they were exposed to the radiation. The monkeys he studied live 50 miles from the nuclear meltdown. He couldn't study monkeys that were closer due to restrictions. (Hayama's findings have been published in the peer-reviewed journal Scientific Reports, published by Nature.) The offspring of exposed monkeys are smaller. They have smaller bodies, much smaller heads, and much smaller brains. It is well known that after Hiroshima and Nagasaki, that fetuses exposed in utero had lower birth smaller heads and brains as well.

Radiation has more intense effects animals with more complicated physiology and faster rate of cellular growth more so than with adult animals. The monkeys exposed also had anemia, less red blood cells, white blood cells, hemoglobin, and bone marrow. The children of Chernobyl suffered similar effects. After retesting throughout the years there has not been any recovery, it is chronic. Birds have also been affected. Many young birds died. White spots turned up on black cows. A type of marine snails vanished, but eventually returned. Fir trees stems are different, weeds grew deformed and thicker. And there is a significant increase of children with thyroid cancer.

The Japanese have done an astounding job. It is heart wrenching that so many lives, human and wildlife were disordered forever because of this calamitous occurrence. The nuclear reactor site held up well to the immense earthquake. But the tsunami and aftershocks, is what truly brought Fukushima to its knees. The impact and weight of the wave was just too much; had they not been so close to shore maybe things would have turned out better. (Note: Some of the data sources for Fukushima are from 2017.)

Public Domain, Map of contaminated areas around the plant (22 March – 3 April 2011) National Nuclear Security Administration (NNSA) US Department of Energy - 4th slide of http://energy.gov/news/documents/AMS_Data_April_4__v1.pptx

The risk that nuclear energy poses to humanity and the planet are not worth it. According to the World Nuclear Association, there are at this time 451 operable civil nuclear power nuclear reactors around the world, with a further 58 under construction. According to EIA (US Energy Information Administration.) There are 61 commercially operating nuclear power plants with 99 nuclear reactors in 30 U.S. states. The question is not, "If?" we will have another nuclear disaster, the question is, "When?" and "Where?".

Some argue the benefits of nuclear energy make the risks worth it. That nuclear energy is virtually clean energy that causes far less pollution than coal. That we should keep it and expand our efforts to build more nuclear power plants. That the reduction in greenhouse gas emissions is so awesome we should put our fears aside, and ignore the pain and suffering caused by the harmful potential long-lasting effects should something go insanely wrong.

We cannot keep burying our heads in the sand. Nuclear energy is not the energy answer for our planet. It's unbelievable to think solar power was discovered in 1839 by Alexandre Edmond Becquerel. The sun is dependable, clean energy. There is only one reason it hasn't taken over as our number one source of energy. It is because of the corporate fat cats that run the government, and own stock in energy corporations. They are payed off to regulate the use of solar energy. In California, even if you have solar panels on your home you still have to give a small payment to the enormous local power company, which has a monopoly on energy in several counties. Humanity needs to fight for more building of free solar energy infrastructure. That is the answer, not the volatile, rightfully controversial nuclear energy power plants.

We know now too well what will happen when we have another nuclear reactor meltdown. Where will the next one be? Which US state will be scarred before humanity takes an international stand against this dangerous energy trend? Nuclear energy is caused by fission. In standard nuclear power plants nuclear fission is used to tear atoms a part. It is scary…what it can do is nothing less than scary. We need to heed history and ban nuclear energy forever; this movement needs to be an international effort. Global action must be taken, to safeguard the planet from anymore nuclear damage. It is going to end up costing more human lives, more animal life, plant life, and more of our precious earth lands and water. Tearing atoms, a part is going to tear our planet apart, if we ignorantly continue the use, and spread of nuclear energy.

# The Historical Use of Fluoride & The Current Controversies Behind It

Stephanie Wolfe

The origins of fluoride are debatable. It has many different forms, naturally occurring and synthetic. This adds to the mass confusion over fluoride. The most early official uses of it can be traced to the UK. The story of how it was implemented for use in the United States is controversial. Studies and financial evaluations suggest it is time for the United States to ban it in public drinking water.

The earliest use of fluoride was in pesticides, to kill roaches, "S. Marcovitch gives some details as to how those fluoride insecticides work (Ind. Eng. Chem. 16 (1924) 1249): "The value of sodium fluosilicate as an insecticide is due to the fact that it is both a contact and stomach poison."

There is a popular belief that fluoride was used by the Nazis, on the Jews in concentrations camps. The first person to first discover the foundation of fluoride was a German man, mineralogist Georgius Agricola, this might have contributed to the Nazi theory. There are also very lengthy articles on the American "fluoride mafia", and the residual sodium fluoride in the air due to early atomic bomb experiments. The "fluoride mafia" allegedly consisted of the most powerful elite families, Ford, DuPont, Rockefeller and more; it is reported that they were responsible in using the American water system as a less costly toxic waste disposal tactic. Sodium fluoride is an industrial byproduct of the manufacturing of phosphate fertilizers.

At one point it was believed to help mineralize teeth, but only in small quantities. In large quantities it actually causes brown stains and discoloration.

Most countries in the world have banned it from public waters. Countries such as China, Israel, Japan, India, and most of Europe label it as a carcinogen, poison, or generally harmful.

The United States claims they originally began adding it to water in New York in 1945, to help poorer citizens especially children save on dental trips. That was before it was available in toothpastes. It cost taxpayers money to put fluoride in public drinking water an estimated dollar per person yearly. Now with so many topical affordable dental care products many advocates against fluoride argue that is simply is no longer necessary to force-medicate the entire population.

China did studies and found that it lowered the IQ of children. Harvard released a study that found it may cause neurotoxicity in laboratory animals, including effects on learning and memory.

It's true that some rodent poisons contain fluoride in them as a main ingredient.

There are four main types of noteworthy fluoride.

There is the naturally occurring 'calcium fluoride' found in soil. In India there is an epidemic of 'skeletal fluorosis' a disfiguring bone disease caused by a buildup of calcium fluoride in the bones. The millions of people who live with this, drink ground water with high amounts of calcium fluoride.

Th next most widely known fluoride is the synthetic industrial byproduct 'sodium fluoride' in its pure form it can eat through concrete and corrode metal. This is what was initially added to water in the USA, and in many states still is.

'Hydrofluorosilicic acid' is another type of popular fluoride that is added to US drinking water; it to is believed to cause learning disorders, ADHD, and weaker bones.

It is worth noting Kentucky has the highest amounts of fluoride in their water and also the highest rate of childhood tooth decay.

There is one other fluoride worth understanding, because of its popular use; 'stannous fluoride'.

The well know dental care company 'Crest' was the first to provide fluoride toothpaste. On their site they explain stannous fluoride, "Stannous fluoride is an anti-bacterial agent that's clinically proven to protect against gingivitis, plaque, and tooth sensitivity, while still providing the trusted cavity protection you expect from Crest." While stannous fluoride might be beneficial for its anti-microbial qualities, it is also proven to cause brown staining of the teeth. So, yes it might prevent tooth decay, but it will yellow the teeth.

There is no valid reason to add any type of fluoride to our drinking water. If one cares to use it, it is available in many different topical products. Too many studies are either inconclusive or point towards data that suggests it harms rather than helps. It's just not worth the millions of taxpayers' money, or the potential risks. The United States should ban it federally, as so many other countries have.

# Prologue to:

# The Doorways of the Mind

Stephanie Wolfe

When I chose the topic hypnosis, I knew nothing about it. I had no argument while doing my research. Whether it would be realistic for more happiness and positive psychology or not. I found some amazing claims and formed my opinion along the way. At times I was against it and at others I was for it. Which felt confusing to me.

I did an experiment with self-hypnosis one night. I was falling asleep, but I grabbed my phone and recorded myself saying positive sentences in the proper hypnotic voice. Things like, "You are smart, and have great ideas. You prefer healthy food to junk food." I listened to it two times, it took about 5 minutes.

Then I fell asleep. In the morning I awoke with an invention idea to help people stay awake on long drives.

"Hmm...That's a great idea," I thought to myself. Was it because of my self-hypnosis? I don't know. Was it because of the simple power of suggestion? Maybe. I have become more attracted to healthier foods, making salads, and choosing fruit more. Coincidence? I wasn't thinking about my experiment at all, I happened to notice well afterwards.

Hypnosis is very interesting, they say we can't be hypnotized to do something we don't want to do...but honestly, I am not sure I believe that. When I did my experiment, it felt eerie. Almost as if the room had changed. It did feel dreamier, fuller somehow.

I did another experiment with a family member who did it on me and then we switched. We did experience time distortion, and I had a flashback to my childhood of something I had not thought about since childhood. Nothing bad just a pretty dress I once had. My family member felt disoriented and disturbed. What is really strange is that we did something very short and basic. But we felt different for several hours. And it made me realize that hypnosis isn't innocent. It may not be "evil" but it's not pointless or innocent at all. It reminded me of something I did as a teen. It felt like the same feeling. Something creepy...Once my friends and I had played with a Ouija board. That's the feeling I can compare it to...it opens a door...a door to something. If our brain is like a car then our conscious mind is the main driver; hypnosis puts that driver to sleep in the backseat and puts the car in cruise control, and the hypnotist is navigating the GPS system, and now the car is driving around inside its own world, not on the streets like everybody else.

It opens that door, and like the third eye opening I am not sure it can ever close. Hypnosis is powerful like a magic wand. It isn't a toy or parlor trick. It is scary, because it seems like something that shouldn't be real, but it is. Intent is important and choosing a hypnotherapist is just as important as choosing who to have sex with, it's extremely intimate and requires perfect trust. There were definitely scary accounts on the internet which I did not use for my report because they were not trusted sources, but still it makes you wonder.

# The Doorways of the Mind

Report on Hypnosis

Stephanie Wolfe

Hypnosis has been around since the 18th century. It has been used in magic routines, medicine, and the occult. Hypnosis conjures up images from corny TV shows in which a spooky voice is used along with a revolving amulet or pendulum. Some say it's dangerous. Some believe it is evil. Is it better to be hypnotized (Hetero-hypnosis.) or is self-hypnosis just as efficient? Can it be used to make us more inclined towards happiness? It is superior or inferior to other attempts humans make to improve their overall wellbeing by increasing the amount of positive psychological flow in our lives? Some say it's ridiculous, impossible, simply a myth. Let us delve into the hypnotic spirals of fact and fiction, by entering the world of hypnosis.

What is hypnosis anyway? Do we have to be asleep, have our eyes closed? The answer is no. Our eyes can be wide open during a trance, and trance is the key word. The trance state is being in a mental zone, in which we are changed by suggestions. But there are layers of this zone. There are light trances and deep trances, and the trained hypnotist knows just how to gently peel away the resistant parts of the conscious mind and get the subconscious mind to come out on the dancefloor with specific sounds and triggers. There are over thirty-one serious techniques. All designed to push aside the conscious will and communicate with the vast space of ethers that holds our memories, our highest hopes, and darkest fears. The 'Relaxation Technique' is one of the more common methods used by therapists and is a basic hypnosis method. Mark Tyrrell a therapist and author clarifies exactly what hypnosis is:

In truth, hypnosis is not inevitably a relaxation state, although it can be. Hypnosis is really a state of highly focused attention. This is what leads to psychological and physical changes. It is very similar to the REM (rapid eye movement) state which governs our dreaming experience while we sleep. So, for example, the experience of physical pain – which is most certainly not relaxing – can nonetheless be extremely hypnotic, because it is so focusing. We are in a highly suggestible state when we are in lust, or frightened, or depressed. These states are emotionally hypnotic, and when we experience them we become more hypnotically suggestible. They are hypnotic states, but not relaxation states.

Relaxation may in itself seem simple, but the difference between relaxation and the relaxation practice is that it leads to the trance state. Once the client is fully relaxed, the next step is the trance state when the mind is opening to suggestion.

Visualization is another serious tenet of hypnosis. It is used to bring about the trance state and to enter suggestions. The hypnotists might ask the subject to recall a memory and describe the room they are in, something familiar at first. To imagine all the fine details of that room; the ground, type of windows, any paintings that are hanging, how it smells? Gradually they move on to fewer familiar spaces, and memories. As the mind struggles with recalling exact details it opens itself to suggestions. Diane Zimberoff, licensed therapist explains the importance of visualization:

Imagining moving a limb, even after it has been paralyzed after a stroke, increases brain blood flow enough to diminish the amount of tissue death. This is a very clear indicator of the power of visualization. Extending the use of hypnosis beyond visualization to incorporate hypnotherapy can be very helpful in assisting a stroke survivor to deal with anxiety and depression that may develop.

So, visualization has a physical effect on the brain and fires up the same section of nerves whether we are doing it or simply seeing ourselves do it! Amazing.

Self-hypnosis is possible as well. Since at least the 1930's there has been much debate and study on the question, "Which is better self-hypnosis or hetero-hypnosis?" Most studies suggest there is no difference, that in a way all hypnosis is a form of self-hypnosis, but there are other studies that have more alarming findings. Adam Eason, a hypnotherapist who has compared many studies states:

In a study of experiential and behavioural differences between self-hypnosis and hetero-hypnosis, Johnson and Lynn (1976) had similar results to Johnson (1979), Johson and Weight (1976) and Fromm (1975). Johnson and Lynn (1976) concluded that self-hypnosis and hetero-hypnosis are indeed similar in most behavioral and phenomenological effects. Additionally, the authors added that hetero-hypnosis evoked more feelings of unawareness, passivity, and loss of control. Self-hypnosis elicited more feelings of time distortion, disorientation, active direction, and trance variability.

In short, self-hypnosis is a bit less risky but is still extremely mind altering and should be approached with great care. A popular method for self-hypnosis is the 'Bodyscan'. We start at the top of the body with our eyes closed, mentally "scan" down slowly from the head to feet. Taking note of every sense, our breathing, what we are lying on, any aches in the body, as the body is stretched out. This is repeated again and again. Scanning up and down until we enter the trance state.

Hypnosis is famous for being mysterious and there are many sceptics out there who either think it's evil, or an illegit form of therapy. There are many web sites mainly by Christians denouncing it. Paul Durbin, United Methodist minister explains, "Hypnosis is mistakenly viewed as mind control or demonic by many misinformed people." Some denominations approve it but with guidelines such as the Roman Catholic church, in 1956 Pope Pius released his permissions carefully:

(1) Hypnotism is a serious matter, and not something to be dabbled in.

(2) In its scientific use, the precautions dictated by both science and morality are to be used.

(3) Under the aspect of anesthesia, it is governed by the same principles as other forms of anesthesia. This is to say that the rules of good medicine apply to the use of hypnosis.

Basically, as long as we are using it for medical reasons and not the devil's work it is acceptable. It is the infamous 'Direct suggestion' that is so controversial. They demand the client do things while in a deep trance state such as, "You will stop smoking." It is this part of hypnosis, that leads people to fear the hypnotist, as this type of therapy demands great care and trust. Intonation of voice is very important in hypnosis, and is used for guidance, direct suggestion, and indirect suggestions. The hypnotist may make suggestions by elongating certain words like, "Relax." or making other more direct words louder such as "Stop." Sometimes strange suggestions are used purposefully to confuse the subject. (Known as the hypnotic art of confusion.) Temporary confusion is said to help the mind eventually, as it induces hyper focus on the voice of the hypnotist, therefore leading to heightened strength to direct suggestions. The official stance about hypnosis is that one cannot be hypnotized into doing something they do not want to do. That is not to say that it is without risks. Hypnosis is a formidable mental tool, and great understanding of it is crucial to be effective, especially if it is to be used for long periods or multiple sessions.

Choosing a reliable and trustworthy hypnotist is important, and the decision to try hetero-hypnosis or self-hypnosis should not be taken lightly.

The act of hypnosis is now being combined with technology such as the 'Easy loss' app. The Easyloss app is a self-hypnosis tool that is supposed to help with cravings and portion control. The app has gained popularity in the UK for bringing about quick results that are long lasting. Choosing an app is a kind of hybrid between self-hypnosis and administered hypnosis, since it gives the client customization control and the ability to read many posts of user feedback experience through online reviews. There are hundreds of different self-hypnosis apps with different goals: self-esteem, ending addictions, positive thinking, ending anxiety, and many of them have high ratings with thousands of users who claim they have had significant positive results.

According to the reviews many of the apps work! Which is rather surprising. Have we really been able to condense centuries of psychological exploration into a tiny app? People are losing weight, ending addictions, feeling more positive about themselves and more in control over their choices conscious and subconscious. In a world full of pain, abuse and suffering hypnosis has the ability to take on the monster in our closets, the dragons we chase, not just in our waking life but in our dreams. It excavates our mental fossils and digs away to find the roots of our deepest issues. Not everyone will need to wield such a commanding sword, some will suffice with more superficial ways to reach that coveted state of flow, but for the traumatized, the abused, hypnosis may be the only thing that truly helps. In cases of great stress, and trauma professional hypnotherapists who specialize in dealing with deeply painful memories should be utilized, for milder problems such as stress relief, or appetite control the hybrid app might actually be just the trick.

# Contact Me

If you would like a copy of my sources please private message me. Thank you for supporting my publications. I have won awards for writing since childhood and have written for the associated press but writing strange historical accounts like these is my calling. I will share with you my personal defenses against the paranormal upon request. I also love helping other writers. I edit for clients and do formatting for them. If you are an amateur writer and would like free feedback on your first chapter contact me at my link below.

https://www.facebook.com/WondermentPublishing/

Printed in Great Britain
by Amazon